The Epigram's Romance

Kalisha D. Lemmitt-Cherry

Peter Cherry

"KDLPC"

Authors: Kalisha D. Lemmitt-Cherry, Peter Cherry Arranger: Peter Cherry, Kalisha D. Lemmitt-Cherry
Copy Editor/Editors: Peter Cherry, Kalisha D. Lemmitt-Cherry
Graphic Designers: Peter Cherry, Kalisha D. Lemmitt-Cherry Cover Art Director and Creator: Peter Cherry
Publisher Angel Concept and Angel Logo by Peter Cherry, Angelic Reign Inc. ® 2004
Interior Simple Design and Artwork Concept Flower by Kalisha D. Lemmitt-Cherry
ISBN: 979-8-9902578-6-3

Table of Contents

Prologue

When an Epigram has an emotional spat with a muse, how would the conversation go?

A Muse

I,
a muse U.
U,
a muse me.
We,
a muse we.
Creatively together;
blending perfectly
in harmony.

Befuddled

Pardon me as I get clean and dress fresh. For
you it's a must; I gotta look my best.
From suits to sweats, more important
personality; because your heart's the best,
I must confess.
Don't you get tired when people obsess over
always putting

people in the better, yet we say place it on yourself ?
Your words say you wanna be with me;
your actions are saying let me go.
I really, really need to know
which is it?
How you make me feel is so surreal like…
Don't you know your sexy?
I don't think you fully understand?
Don't you know if you're ready?
I think you should fully comprehend.
I want to feel it! The miracles you do from within is rated top ten, beautiful.
Outside; and just sexy; can have a freak nasty mind.
I can still be your friend.
Unfortunately, if you think you get stuff just because you cute
you truly missed a lesson. Then if you got a ugly heart with no hugs
then that just means a two out of ten.
I'll be afraid if you go.
I'm afraid if I continue to stay.
I'll be afraid if you leave me.
Oh, where would my heart go so many emotions this evening.

Hook with no verse

I got a hook with no verse
Oh, my goodness gracious.
I don't have the words to say.
Oh, my goodness gracious.
What if,
I don't have words to play?
Oh, my goodness gracious.
I got a hook with no verse
I can't find my pen.
I can't find my paper.
I can't find anything.
Oh, what a caper.
All of these things
are so essential.
What room is this pencil?
Oh, well alright.
I'll even write on this stencil.
Not even a crayon within my
grasp; I sit and I laugh
until it's contagious.
Outrageous.
Oh, my goodness gracious.
I got a hook with no verse

If I had no
money in my pocket.
If I had some
money in my pocket.
Will I have some luck?
Will I have some love?
Or, it's just a tool?
And, I'm just a fool?
To think that dollars
buy happiness;
it's up to you.
Keep growing.
Believe in you.
Keep going.
I'm believing in me.
Keep learning.
We believe in us.
Goodness gracious.
Keep loving.
We believe in the world.
May we come together as
one heart.
I got a hook with no verse in this motha fucka babe.

A Funny Story

So me and my man was talking about spicing up the bedroom.
So let me tell ya.
Went to this freak shop and got some handcuffs.
I wanted the pink fuzzy ones; but he was like those looked
like feathers would be everywhere.
"And I'm allergic," he said.
"Okay; so let's get the regular steel ones," I said.
"These are good," said the clerk, pointing to a metallic pair.
Damn, he was nosy. "Okay then; let's get these." We
agreed on the opposite pair--- the stainless steel. Plus
it won't rust.
"Ooh, look at these."
I held up some orange glittered nipples clamps.
"Hmm…," my Man thinks about it, and said, "For you not me."
I loved his one liners.
Keeps me in check and hot all at once.
'Oh, those are super complicated," interrupted the clerk.
"I tried those with my second girlfriend, and she told my wife
that she had sore nipples for a month. Mistress didn't
mind though,' continued the clerk.
Whoa! TMI.
We passed on those.
After ten minutes we decided on the handcuffs,
a whip, and the nipple clamps with the chains.
'Have fun. Lemme me know how it goes,' said the clerk.
"Yea; right ," said my Hubby.
He was fed up with this dude.
"Uh, no," I agreed.
We left.
The ride home was fun. I even drove.
He held the bag of goodies like a bag of assorted penny candy.
Anxiously, he kept looking in the bag. We both couldn't wait to try the
treats. After settling in at home, we inspected our inventory.
But didn't use it.
We didn't need it.
The experience in the sex shop (minus the clerk) was enough.
Funny thing was just the act and not the action made the bedroom spicer.

Per’La Mae

Per’La Mae open up the door babe!
It's 3’o clock and this key ain’t
working because this lock saying other
thangs.
You think I was out there with
Big ass Bir’da; smoke in the air
turning like circles.
Why you tripping on me, Babe?
She said,
"Oh La-di -da
La-di-da
La-di-da
Oh La-di -da
La-di-da
La-di-da."
Per’La Mae
I ain’t doing nothing babe
It’s 4 o’clock
sleeping in the car
not working, plus
the neighborhood saying
other thangs. Just because
I was chilling with Big ass Bir’da
smoke in air turning like circles
why you tripping on me babe!
She said,

"Oh -la - di-da
La - di – da
La- di - da
Oh - la -di-da
La-di-da
La -di-da."
Per'La Mae
I'm tired and hungry.
It's 5 o'clock and
I gotta be at work soon
but dealing with you
saying other thangs.
I guess I'll be
at Big ass Bir'da's.
Got my clothes
thrown from the
window, turning like
circles.
Is it you, or is it me
babe? And she said ,
"Oh La - di -da
La - di-da
La - di -da
Oh la -di - da
La-di-da
La-di-da."
Let me in the babe.
She said nope.

Word

While grabbing cucumbers and tomatoes
to chop up for a salad,
the Gentleman is talking to his Lady about his work day.
He said, "Baby ain't got time for games.
Baby, I ain't gonna complain."
She said, "Baby, I know.
I don't like games, either.
Always got time for honesty.
What would you like for dinner?"
He said back,
"Rather be working and making money."

She said, "This has been a week!
Baby, we both need to relax and eat.
After dinner, you can go back to work.
I got a good book to read."
She holds up this book.
After looking at the cover, he said,
"To be honest, let's skip dinner and be some freaks.
I want you to read to me."

Book Mo Build

Books;
Books; and more
Books.
That's all I want to collect.
I want books stacked higher than
I can reach; but not too far from my fingertips.
I want books in volumes, books in collections.
Stacked neatly against the wall by the fireplace.
I can't wait for more books!
Books on the window sills about windmills.
Books about education.
Books about vegetation.
Books by writers and poets.
About mystical beasts and boats.
Most important, definitely books by me and you!
Writing the bestsellers
and being book sellers!

Read

If people would
spend more time
reading books
than people,
the world may be
a better place.

Enchanted Water Falls

I got lost in your enchanted waterfall.
Chilling with no bliss, just in love, with no care at all.
No forget me nots, no roses; poor romance
inside a crowded club.
All alone in a dance, no one speaks of love; but
lust is still popping in a velvet tub with no cares; I guess
disenchanted by a hopeless romantic.
I got love for sale, not the physical, but the emotion itself.
I got the finest elixir you can't get nowhere else.
Welcome to my passion factory.
I got lost in your enchanted waterfall
Chilling with no bliss, just in love, with no care at all.
Twirling my Parasol,
it's been a weekend season since we even danced at all.
I was wondering how within a week,
you and I could do it all under a lovely?
As I fall in my notion's potion, glimpse
of heart's motion connecting
or, should I stay alone graciously
because you don't care at all?
I got lost in your enchanted waterfall.
Chilling with no bliss, just in love, with no care at all.

Love

Holding me.
Rubbing me.
Loving me-eee.
Just said I want you-u (Oo)
And you said you want me-e (too)
Just to be in your presence
Makes me, myself, and I so jealous.
All vying for your time.
Oooh you always on my mind.
(And I know)
When I see you.
(That we)
Are meant to be.
(So come here)
And whisper in my ear.
Baby I love you-ou-ou.
I'll whisper in your ear.
Baby I love you-ou-ou.

Truly Love

Sadness falls;
emotional rain hits
my windowpane
within my tears drops.
So, if you catch my love
hold it close, please.
Good days I think I failed,
because bad days
got the best of me.
If you pursue my heart,
please approach it slowly.
I've been hurt
and lonely so long.
If you pursue my heart
please love me truly.
I've been hurt and lonely so long.
My love truly, truly love.
My love truly truly love.
Drifting into the notion
of a love warm and cozy,
my heart been sailing;
cold and lonely.
So, if you pursue my heart,
please approach it slowly;
it's been hurt and lonely for so long.
If you pursue my heart,
please love me truly.
My love truly, truly love; my love truly; truly
love.

Untitled

In your head, or in your heart,
the voice of love lets one know their part.
What part is theirs or what others expect.
Sometimes love can leave
the pillow cold with tears;
wet drops; hiccups thunderous
like three days of a weathered storm.
In your head and heart, the reason of love
should let one know their part.
Sometimes, love leaves aches and pleasure.
Tears of pain.
Lust regained.

Funk and loans (Gone get it)

Gone get it. Gone get it. Gone get it. Gone get it.
The scratch got us paid, the dough made the credit better.
The bread got us eating, bankrupt mind is a never clever.
Financial intelligence can last forever.
What do you know in increasing in your cheddar?
No worries; bank notes shows financially carefree.
No pressure calls from creditors, or is it just me?
Turned up to chill out at a hundred degrees.
Lately it's been crazy, or somewhat way ridiculous.
Who would have predicted a season so relentless?
Aye, I ain't got time to waste! Show me the figures of facts
or you get the hell up out my face
My mind is in a new zone. (Not that bullshit)
Show me the bankroll. You've been a dollar short all along
That's what's your selfish ass is; all alone
hard head, soft ass ET looking call home.
Not answer from anyone. Because everyone all gone.
Gone get it. Gone get it. Gone get it.
Sometimes, I rant when I work. Always handling business.
Balancing personal life should be on everyone's wish list.
I'm kicking opinion, or is it just fact? My portfolio
won't be under attack. Run it back.
We just told you how to increase your stacks.
Clear mentality. Probably, obviously
the world in a state of decay. Ain't got no time
for the negativity; keep that bullshit away. Peace
and love to you is just a mindset away.

Found

You found it; but, it wasn't even missing.
It was hiding.
Yet, it was where it was supposed to be.
However,
you were being you and too busy to see.
Take time to enjoy life and its moments.

On My Writer's Block

Avoiding thinking and paper glancing at every chance
and I get nothing but a blank wall
looking back at me.
I stare at it so hard
and then work up a nerve to lower my guard;
and put pen to paper to write a scenario with some sense.
Making a rhyme out of a visional pattern.
Making a story out of a open mind.
I look then glance around at the environment;
everyone everywhere and over there.
I can finally see
because it all can tell a story.
Now the brick wall of my
writers block can break free
from my mind.

Love Note

Trying to think of so much to say,
but sometimes minds don't think that way.
So, I'm writing you this love note.
And really hope that it excites your day.
Trying to write the words to say,
but sometimes pens don't write that way.
So, I'm writing you this love note.
Can wait for it to excite your day.

Soulatic Pulsar

I can stretch a sun beam
all the way to two weeks
from today.
I brought the sun and moon together
just so night can play with day.
I put the stars in the sky
to capture the twinkle
in your eyes.
Now with those same eyes,
just blink three times;
look at your hands, find
a diamond, sapphire, and onyx.
I do this not to show off;
just to show how much I love you
sincerely and honest.

Softest

if this is how
one makes
you feel,
you get it;
but words
can strike one.
feelings 10x deeper.
do you really feel
the softest of the punctuations?

1 up groove

What color is Love?
What color is life?
What color is believing?
Does it even matter?
Because without it, it's just
the coldest of nights.
Even when I'm awake
I think I'm dreaming.
I can't believe what I'm seeing.
The world is on
fire and no one believing.
They think I'm insane for this.
Reason: I speak my heart, and
for that it's treason?
Just another example of the coldest
season.
What's the color of love?
What's the color of life?
What's the color of pain?
What's for the color of strife?
Are we just painting by numbers, or we just free
styling?
Creating strokes in our life; better wake the what up.
From the hype check yourself; make sure your spirit
right.
To admire all colors is like artistry in bloom.
Yet to trip on all cultures?
Really, what's the matter with you?

Sage

Open a window
Light it up.
Let that foolishness go.
Be free.
Fan it.

Say it.
Sway it.
Wave it.
Circle around with it, like the wind.
Obtain that peace.
There are those who never run wild with the wind.
Just because the wind is moving east, then is it a lie?

Oceanmatic

I'm the author of my context metaphor far more than you
accept. The irony of nothing more or nothing less.
Got me putting oxymoron's in a supplex because I'm vexed.
My mood imperative; tone indefinite.
Chill flow, impeccable knowledge melodic.
Like an exotic erotic with a topic I'm Oceanmatic.
With my vocab I'm a chef. In the kitchen with
the beats, I'm a mad scientist. In the lab and
it's hitting; forehead glistening.
So underground I'm probably the only one who's listening.
My own rhymes are writing on the floor to ensure it is
hardcore.

Say What?!

People like pawns
that eat prawns
under an umbrella covered patio
on the street waiting
for cool people to meet.
Can't start the show, honey
if no one put the batteries
in the remote
to control the theme.
You get so used to somethings
that your toes taps the remix
every time the world
seems to lose its mind.
You can divide 100 by 5
and still end up
with 20 every time.
Dress up in the world
wearing the finest diamonds and pearls
but to undermine the matters of the heart
by being a shell
of oneself
is fucked up…
But say it again?
Say what?!

(Insufficient Funds Card Insufficient)

I know you ain’t tripping; you can miss me with that.
This thing gotta be kidding; you can miss me with that.
This machine got my money and it won’t give it back.
Where are my receipts at,
I could have sworn I had enough stacks.
All I did was buy me a golden plane,
bought a diamond castle with the latest everything.
Had a boat made out of pearls; dated a mermaid
she got mad and had to watch it sink.
Just thinking about I got a bottle of…
‘Whatever it’s called’, all I know it’s $500.00 to drink.
Fifteen women in my life, so I bought their ass are pink.
That soft thread count was mink.
Now this machine is acting
nutty; there’s a long line behind
me now saying, "Hey, buddy."
Damn.

Dance

You make me sing, baby.
You make me dance, sugar.
You make me sing,
la la la la la la la la-la-la.

You make me see you, baby.
You make me hear you, baby.

You make me sing,
la la la la la la la la-la-la.
You make this feel
like a slow groove,
with loving grind,
la la la la la la la la-la-la.

Theme Parks and Funnel Cake

K.I. S.S I love it when you R.I.D.E on me.
Just the taste of your ice cream you keep my roller coaster so busy.
While your cotton candy water park feels so nice.
I can't help myself I go back more than twice.
This grown funk groove is what we like, Babe.
Your love is like theme parks and funnel cake.

Like two thrill rides on our crazy ferris wheel;
with the attitude of whatever so I had,
to let you know; about all that love from you.
Your love is like theme parks and funnel cake.
Floating in your love tunnel, rocking like bumper cars;
while I'm eating my cake with ice cream;
roller coaster melting all on your face. I want my babe.
All I need is my Lady. My favorite song; you are my favorite song. Your love is like theme parks and funnel cake.

Artist

I've painted portraits of us in my mind.
A gallery filled of passions and desires.
My love
the tingle of our spines

when we intertwine…
so dramatic…
Our charisma so energetic.

You wow me.
I wow you.
I woo you.
you woo me.
Together, we create
a masterpiece.

Graceful graciously

Tasting the concept of love I want to sample your aura.
I want to place your soul in situations
That when you look in the mirror your spirit
refers to you as bougie as you laugh
while inspiration kiss your lips.
Making your inner yearning wanna suck.
May I taste your tits, slow dancing with you
rubbing on hips and cheeks
I want to go in between loving you softly
with my dick so hard.
It's something about good ass women with good ass pussy.
I understand how wonderful communication
can be it's a cool ass trip.
Lost in this vibe by far I will conclude by saying
I am the rocket-ship and you are my star.

Late Night Snack

He was watching tv slightly.
I heard him snore.
So I got up out the bed and headed for the living room door.
There he was on the sofa looking so fucking good
he was lying there dick in his hands
all I wanted to do was get it out of his pants
so I moved forward and gently rested on my knees
I didn't want to wake him up until I do what I please
moistens lips tight hips pussy all a blaze
been wanting to give him head all day anyway
I pull the dick out out it was a slight drip out off
the grey sweatpants that he wore I tore into the dick all
while rubbing my clit made him come he looked at me
I swallowed then I licked we both fell back exhausted.

Cutey

She cute we all use that excuse because she was just spotted in this club
dropping it too many miles to turn and just go back now already drove.
just walked up in this place and now she's ready to go now
She's ready to roll out now just remember what the ol' people said
Now she's doing things that she said she would never do.
My curiosity is gone I'll talk to you later.
I only been with her for three weeks and I'm pretty much sure I think I hate
her. I mean I just dislike and disagree with her on how I should cater.
To her
It's only been three weeks she thinks I should buy her a purse.
I'm like I'm a just getting to know ya and ain't you a nurse.
Then she had the audacity to curse.
A argument starts and right know her attitude is like an argent fart.
Damn chick you moving too quick .
What if I said off the bat when you gonna suck my dick.
Then what next week I'm stuck in some legal shit.
So tonight I tip my hat don't worry a bit
I'm out the door cause your aura a trip
just a little bit.
Bitter wilted vintage socialite
Now she's doing things that she said she would never do.

Need

Sometimes, I need it.
Give it to me now!
I can't wait.

Come here.
Now.
What did you say?
Come closer…
So, I can hear you.
Feel you.
And, at last,
taste your love.
I need it,
and you

want it, too?
Yes?!
Oh, so wonderful!

Question

Are your thoughts
of a love utopia gone?
Thanks to the inventions,
and the, “see me-hear me” types,
and privacy and peace
are no longer.
Love should be the main thing.

Banter

Here is a little story about the squirrel; the bunny, and the
bird. Fuck what ya heard because this shit muggy!
Quickly… somebody hug me!
I'm crafting this narrative maybe
you could be mad at me,
and say you don't love me
They falling out trying catch words,
but that stack was heavy trying to understand
on a shaken up levy
and I'm too heavy you left me.
Sad and alone in this house.
I'm so confused in doubt trying to figure shit out
My heart aches like my baby toe hitting
the edge of the couch
I'm yelling out but damn it!
"I can't leave the house," said the
squirrel to the bird and bunny.
"And I'm out."

Daydream

I thought I was writing, yet I was
sitting; and somewhat daydreaming.
A visualization of us holding hands,
leaves me in a wet bliss.
I find myself startled with hot desire.
I walk within the middle of love's pathway.
A little bit around and down, further I find you.
Pen in hand; writing the next soul stirring monologue,
while saying sweet soliloquies.
About you and me?
I rush to you to embrace you,
but you vanish in front of my face
I'm left with only your cologne's lavender's trace.
I feel a touch of cold upon my shoulder,
then I feel the touch of warm hands upon my face
As you kiss me out of my daydream.

Balloon Message

I wrote you this letter
and tied it to a balloon;
and I hope this message
gets to you very soon.
I never claimed to be perfect even for me.
It's a nice thought, though but it wouldn't fit.
I'm growing within me; working hard ;always cool, and talking shit.
Praying to the Lord to always hold me.
I am me; at least I know who I am.
I wrote you this letter
and tied it to a balloon;
and I hope this message
gets to you very soon.
It's just nuts for the question of merely us.
Out of our minds, the crying intellectual children
of bitter roses and anxiety won the decadence.
I guess you can say I got a two-sided view of our
personal behavior, what is in ignorance.
I capture self-exile, for my eyes keep seeing a rapture.
God bless you; I'm alone either way.
Oh' why anxiety this ain't the way it supposed to be
or is it just the ravings of me in stereotypes?
Antiquated just so to heal my heart; love up;
and never give up and when it comes right down.
So, if you're on bullshit, don't expect me to be around.
I doing us all favor. So;
I wrote you this letter
and tied it to a balloon and I hope this message gets to you very soon.

Talk

The mood is melancholy and one is chilling.
Upon the motions, and notions for silences.
Neither deprive nor divide the attention from the feelings of,
'huh' derived from the voice of 'quietness'.
Yet, sit satisfied to know that one was in control and constant.
The truth paused yet still moving in the mind.
Trying to figure out what is left behind.
Feelings of void and unwant
or, to want to speak because
one is always listening patiently,
but, wanting to not only listen, but be heard instead
of being shushed.
And for a moment one's eyes
of bewilderment heat up
But the soul is still warm at the heart
And a tear shall not part from the eye
Love so much between the two,
just talk about it.

Feeling Hurt

I never want to see your eyes in sorrow.
I'm looking across the other way I'm in a void called '
"For what the hell?" is this season of heartache.
Miscommunication blocking pathways that true.
Got us questioning moments of bloom or
were they simply moments of doomed love in despair.
I would like to provide you a towel for this damp night.
I'm the one that watch in the moonlight instead of the
spotlight. I can tell the mood is not right; everyone up tight.
Evenings never forget your own light; wittiness
feeling nice all right. Still blessed.

Life

Even when it's muddy and dark;
wonderful lovers should always
have pleasurably walked in the park.
When days get cloudy,
and even when walking through life's mazes;
Together,
both can see exactly where the directions go,
and how to keep moving within this life together.

Legitimate Mirror

Retracing my steps; wondering how our
conversation went left. Then, I took a deep breath.
Looked in, and said fuck it.
My words absurd?
I've always been criticized and it seems
my doubters can't look directly in my eyes! Damn.
First time, I arrived too early.
Second time, I came on time.
Third time, I tickled your fanny.
Fourth time, I blew your mind.

The love we got insane now, babe.
Lady, slide over here and peep my game.
Let's have a conversation and I bet with you
I'll do the same. Will this conversation prove how
much I feel about you by omission?
I can only adore you from a distance.
Sitting alone by myself; second
guessing what else.

Windy

The world is winded
and the outside has ended.
Freedom was water you roamed
on the shores of your being in your mind.
Trying to find an understanding and healing.
Trying to focus on your, mines, and our feelings.
Knowing that love and conversation
was the only thing you and I are needing
.

Application Attendee

You need someone to believe in; better look inside of
you. God graced us all with gifts; better use it
before you lose believe it.
Go on; this is your moment; grab it get like you want
it. Give all you got ;this is your moment.
Life ain't what you want it to be.
Aye, attendee.
Life can be what you want it to be.
If you want happiness in your life,
you gotta get to that inner love.
Keep cultivating that to reach that higher love.
Know that the option, it resides in you.
It resides in me. How you feel?
Feeling good.
To be of the be a forward thinking attendee.

Going

The double vision kicked in
I fell down like bowling pins.
I thought I wan't able to get back up.
BUT I am able to keep leveling up!
Rebalancing myself; knowing that I
was always there,
for I had never left;
my love and sweet gentleness

like gentle sunbeams.
For my world is filled with so much more.
It wasn’t so less enough.
And yes, it’s been tough
and others probably have it too much
However, I know I keep going.

Universe

This should be the second stanza:
Wonderment and amazement.
We loved for days and it turned into an eternity.
I want to be where we are.

By far my love your better than the best.
By far my love your as sweeter than it gets
By far my love you are the sun moon and the stars….
You want to be where we are.

Wonderment and amazement.
Our loved for days is an eternity.
Wonderment and amazement..
We love always and eternity.
We want to be where we are.

By far, love's just to come.
By far love's song to be hummed.
By far the love radiates to the sun the moon and the stars.
U-n-i
Universe.

Rain

Here it comes!
Here it comes!

The rain!

Oh, rain!

Here it comes,
Oh, rain!
Rising umbrellas and newspapers.
Falling hair and faces.
Jumping over puddles.
Tripping about no sunshine.
Why such the rush?
Why so unhappy?

It's just rain.
Need the sun? But the rain is here, okay?

Let it touch your skin like a lover's tongue.
The wetness resting all upon you.
When you 'cum dry
You will be refreshed again.

Falling in lavender

I stood in utter amazement as she touched a rose petal so
subtlety stroking her fingernails suddenly changing its
color demonstrating her power of manipulation.
I'm falling in lavender.
I stand in the the marvel of her majesty.
She looked upon me smiled and winked.
If she read my mind I don't know what she's think.
I'm falling in lavender .
Passionate bloom is brash and refreshing;
searching for inner peace taking on the
everyday situations .I'm falling in lavender.
Drama, inspiration, pain and love with unapologetic
hugs.
I'm falling in lavender
"I love to make a grown woman blush."
Authentic, she ain't even trying to rush.
Immature minds missed the bus.
All I'm saying it's cool
let's conversate about us falling in
lavender. Lovely, what you doing to me?
I'm falling in lavender.
Anything you want from me.
I'm falling in lavender .
Oh, is this where love could be I guess?
I'm falling in lavender.
She had me in a trance using the
silk fan in her hand in the other

was bushels of lavender that had
Life on the band or maybe even a string
she asked me for waltz and said
“Do you believe in dreams”?
I replied it depends on overall message it brings
She said "What about the minor things?
My retort, "Is their such a thing?"
She said, "I kinda like you."
From her lips ,she placed a kiss as calming as
lavender. Or, is it I just smitten. Falling in
lavender.

Taut

I was sitting just thinking;
minding my business;
trying to wind down for the evening.
Yet you came into the room,
with you taut body and nakedness.
I couldn't help but to stare
and stopped minding my business
The thought to place
you upon my chin.
My lover, I grinned as I look up at
you.
Finest specimen of a man.

Wanted

Wanted:
skin to skin;
grin to grin.
Baby,
we are a win.
Thank you.
You're welcome.
Being open, never wanting to hide.
All in this skin; in this musical melody
of poetry; prose; art; and music.
Lovelorn, hot loins, and passionate kisses.
Good eats and good treats.
Laughs abundance.
Conversations upon us.
Electric duo.
So alive.
Love you.

Lickable

A hot kiss to moist lips our tongue slow dance while we dip.
Around the room as we sip on sensual.
Freaks, you and me tasting songs of lovers' funk.
I gently thrust into your womb, with you wanting the full bass of the boom. Lady, you have me while you're throwing back the boom of the bass. You barely have anything on but some lace.
After one night of pleasure, the next morning you're sitting on my face.
I can tell you're self as hell for you could not wait until I was fully awake.

Silken Dreams

To me,

you are more
than just a fantasy.
Not a daydream
but a restful night

that keeps me

in silken dreams.

Gotten

She's intelligent laid-back lavishly lovely;
so sexy looking she got me so in love.
I can't wait t to see my lady who has my
heart. She loves it when I sweet talk even;
when I decide to gift her a necklace just few inches
below of her breast and cotton candy heart clouds in bliss.
I'm a mess; give me a kiss.

Shit, I know; but I will freak you best no more nothing
less.

Pleasurable Eroticism

Pleasurable eroticism.
What is your-ism?
What is it that makes your fantasy?
Do you want to be nasty?
Climb the wall
of ecstasy?
Or, be nice
and lick it up.
Love is a high.
And sometimes it's a price.
But if you want a piece of action.
Pleasurable eroticism is what your asking.
In a book.
On the air.
You would like your pleasurable eroticism where?
Release and be free to talk dirty.
Without being judge.
Maybe sexual energy is part of your grudge.
Sometimes people need a nice warm body.
To keep them from getting colder.
This groove is for the 40 and older..
We can talk about it shouldn't older age make us bolder

Melt yourself and let me be your mold.
Come on now it's okay.
Isn't that why you came to play?
Pleasurable eroticism all day.
Did you hear what I said?
Oh, no not over the rocking of the bed.
I guess I feel and bumped your head.
Pleasurable eroticism is the -ism.

Pleasurable eroticism is what is needed .
Pleasurable eroticism even I need it. Mentally,
physically, or emotionally.
Pleasurable eroticism for you and for me.

Never Knew

The winds of change made us a strain.
I know more about you from miles and miles
away than I ever knew you when you were in my face.
Am I out of place to give an apparent constructive critique?
Then, if just a shadow of residue of you thinking of me, but
by now I can't even recall your name.
I would say then you, "Please tell me all my mistakes."
Simply;
someone I never
knew.

Chill

I may get on your nerves. (Sometimes)
You may get on my nerves. (Well, sometimes)
We do give each other grace (Always!)
Cuz, I love yo ass soo much! (Kisses!)
In my soul and in my flesh. (Oh!)
I always give you the best. (Damn right!)
Fuck the rest! (Yeap!)
Yea, I said it with my chest. (And, will say it again!)
So come here. (Please!)
Let's chill out. (I'm on my way!!!)

Thanks for asking

I’m an addict for your adulation.
My mind's a rapid rabbit and my pen is the dangling karat. This what I’m going through. I’m stressed out without the sadness monster obstacles madness. It’s a habit, I just need to sit back and start relaxing. Other than that, I’m fantastic.

Yes

What is it that you require?
Hot wishes with lustful desires?
Abundance of kisses?

Sexy dances from your misses?
Hot meal with a cold drink?
Tell me, what do you think?
About what it is that you need?
I will give you x,y, z, one, two, three,
and everything in between.
Just to let you know how much you mean
to me.

Feeling of Moments

She said; “Damn you got hard!”
I replied; I know.
You got me day dreaming I’m literally tripping now.
I’m visualizing about last night feasting upon your pie.
Wow!
Looking in your eyes I start to fantasizing about being freaky outside.
While we puffing on a cloud sipping on a waterfall with the lights down.
She gripping my stick I feeling inside her interior walls.

Ring Around

Of course you can get it
No hestiation
So in love with you
You're more than a ring around my finger, Husband.
Forever in this space, I am Wife.
All up in your face
With wet kisses
Giving everything that's been missing
Always glad to be your MRS.
(thank you having me)

Illuminate Night

Let's illuminate the night!
What does basking in love it feel like?

I wanna know are you afraid to ponder the notion?
Illuminate the night!
What does love feel like?

Is it like the four-letter word lust?
Feeling can be debated or argued; too toxic.
I got more four-letters even better for your eyes.
You're not afraid of the us that's so mature.
Illuminate the night
Maybe we can make the sun come out.

I’m blessed as me

I still got struggles you see humanly standing here with my heart on my sleeve
while I’m emotionally naked sometimes I feel like can’t be protected.
Anxiety with every cry feels like I’m neglected.
Just because I disagree.
I’m aware of the bad times I’m aware of the bullshit
I could rather explode or choose not to even invest in the stress.
With the nonsense it possesses when I was younger,
I looked in the mirror and found out the biggest enemy is me versus myself
Anyone else’s bullshit just was scavenging in the wake of what was left what I had left. Now like anyone my feelings are valid and that’s how I felt.
Now Maturity and wisdom changed my subliminal and spiritual depth.
So now I wanna well wish everyone prosperity and health.
My mind and voice has to constantly be contested.
You going to teach me; “You lesson”! Is it the question?
Or is it the answer in the story of life we all play the part of lancer.
What if I was to say I didn’t care about you.
I would be amiss our hearts are exposed
who the he’ll wants to take a risk
I’m sending likability unsealed with a kiss.)
Enough of me what about you. Aye!
You got stress in your life congratulations so do I.
Sometimes I wanna fight; wanna cry; wanna dance
Shiiiit! Heaven forbid the twisted side.
How about another alternative relax and vibe to
whatever you like as long it truly heals what ill inside.
Cause your spirit to do a flip every time you allow yourself to be.

Creative

All I got is creativity.
Sometimes I wonder if that's all I know.
I wonder if I had too much knowledge to show.
I wonder what is behind the next closed door.
However,
I've got creativity.
That's all I know.
But, I think I know too much.
My mind works in a clutch of the hand
of a bright, neon yellow watercolor pencil
Then, I have to pause on what it is to be done;
and try not to become restless with this resistance
of always needing and wanting to creative MORE.
All I got is creativity
Sometimes, I wonder if I'm creating enough.

Tales

What's has become of us?
Surviving, we keep telling the tales.
Trying to do well,
and being chill.
Just sitting here, working and existing.
Wonder it anyone is listening,
Instead of trying to tell us what
we did wrong to the younger generation.
Like a hopeful sunray, or delightful moon,
from the sky above;
are these worlds of heaven on Earth?
Wading through time will only tell.
Some thoughts create our voice so well.

To survive, we keep living to tell the tales.
What has become of the?
We survived to keep living to tell the tales.
A lot of people come and gone
back home to glory.
Some many things changed and spinning
around like red ball with silver Jaxs,
Places with horrific sidewalk shadows
of former brick and mortars;
abandoned schools;
and patchy parks;
Some once fine creations
Some once in our heyday
Hey!
We're all still here;
just must keep on living to tell the tales.

Naïve bucket

My heart has scars from remnants of past relationships torn apart.
Denial of it’s not being love at all perhaps I was the one who is naïve.
Everyone else was in true love withdrawal
the possibly was just there moments.
Loves has a pain that will make your emotions run a miles
away just to break the glass of propaganda.
I guess everyone perfected what I couldn’t understand.
I dared lied to say I didn’t care to pacify I don’t understand.
I wasn’t the one I wasn’t hope love and peace to you just
a toy puppy or panda kind of outlander.
Know I’ll be on my way. That’s all right; that’s
okay. I wasn’t the one you was tripping on anyway
That’s it; that’s all right that’s okay.
I understand it was fun while it lasted.
I wasn’t the one you wanted any way got to go bye.

Do It

Do it like I told ya.
No questions; just do it.
What did you come here for?
What is your question again?
I have you the command.
You got the right answer.
It was word for word.

Instruction by instruction.

So do it like I told ya.
Even if you disagree
Or, have a thought of your own.

.

Love me or leave me

I would rather stand in line all day
than sitting here arguing with you.
I'd rather drive a sleigh on a summer day
than sitting here arguing with you.
I would rather change a tire in the rain
than sitting here arguing with you.
I rather read a book about some
string than sitting here arguing with
you. Love me or leave me alone!
Where is you're mind at, please let me know!
Yes!
Your mindset; I'm just asking because I'm too busy for that
BS. I ain't got time to invest in that mess.
Look a here, babe.
My world has been spinning differently lately.
Maturity has been following me around, and just maybe.
I decided in relationships, I can't deal with one sided!
Bad vibes I don't need it!
Reduction of drama and negativity needs to repeated rather
than just ignore and hide it. I just decided to face it
at this time.
I wanna cry ; in pain and heart ache.
I'm in hurt; why would I lie?
Just know even with tears
dwell strength upon my eyes.
I felt negativity vibes Instead of
allowing myself to get lost in the dark

I allowed myself to provide some light.
Everyone in the world is going through something.
Even though I'm doing something.
I feel like I'm not doing enough of something which sometimes I
feel like I'm not doing nothing.
On me.
All of this panic ain't helping too much;
along with too much and too little social consumption.
Got me feeling off kilter.
I gotta stop self-judging and get a handle on why.
I'm tripping; I need to get some fresh air take a walk or
something. This is the get up after being knocked down there is a
replacement. My life's not perfect; so you're deflection
is not my protection. What the hell do you want me.

Grow

Just like you,
a plant can grow so much.
And, sometimes, within in a bunch.
When it spreads and out grows the pot,
it's had too much;
and ready to go.
Then you know you need to
get to the root,
cut the cord,
separate,
and explore.

It’s What Ever

Sun just came up shining so bright
it’s a little windy but the temperature feel nice.
Earlier, I ate and showered; catching the tail end of the night.
Got dressed fresh, but I’m still about comfort alright.
I even saw something so cool and unique. Animals
can talk to each other, 'cause I saw a squirrel shaking
it’s head when a bird next to it went tweet-tweet.
They probably was talking about what happened far;
just away from them; about twelve feet.
Two of the neighbors dogs, Wheeler and Zeke
getting into it with some coyotes that escaped from the zoo
Damn, it’s tough up in these streets.
Well, this is not about to let me leave and proceed on my
way, even in that moment. If nobody believes me about this
fray; it's cool and it didn’t mess up my day.

Bye

Oh no! Leave your bullshit behind!
You can come on relax.
Even take off your shoes.
You can leave them at the door
But if you're bringing bullshit
you can go back outside the door.
Get back in your in your car
and drive back to your house.

It All Make Sense

Walking down the block one day,
a dog-walker overheard a conversation coming from the front
porch of an old house down shaped like an old brown,
dirty top hat with windows that look like eyes into one's soul.
The old lady on the porch in the rocking chair said,
"Lemme tell you!
I ain't got nothing for you,
cuz you ain't never had nothing for me!
Everything I gave was for free,
but yet love seemed to have a price for me!
You see
don't know who it is
don't care who it is
negativity
can't get through my door."
Her neighbor, an Old Man, was holding a garden hose
and watering the sand outside of his house that looks like
a genie lamp with green lights said,
"People ain't what they cracked up to be
You think because they are....to you
That these fools are a true blue.
Naw, they don't mean it at all.
But always want you to to be the first to
call. Well, forget them all ;
don't know who it is;

don’t care who it is;
negativity
can’t get through the door, either.”
He pointed back to his house.
The dog-walker waved to them.
They waved back.
Old Lady said, “Hey, you there!”
The dog-walker stopped and glanced.
“Remember,
some people aren’t so happy.
Hope ya happy with what
couldn’t be bought in a store.”
Old Man replied,
“Love and happiness
should hold so much more.
Freedom, love and light
is what we’re still looking for."
“Damn! Thanks for that insight!”
The dog-walker went back home and
decided to give real love a chance.
Love is not about what it bought and given
but what comes from the heart.
Sometimes, we all just need a place to start.

Da Bush

"Oh, my goddesses!"
"What!"
"I lost the bush!"
"What"?!
"I repeat; I lost the bush!"
"How could you lose a bush?!"
"Funny you mentioned that." I mention, with slight embarrassment.
"Well, remember when you asked me to water the bushes?"
" Yea."
"Well, I had too much berry juice, and had to drain mine."
The group slaps their foreheads. "Then, when I came back, it just vanished."
"My bush is on the loose everyone quickly we must grab my bush!"
"Beware of, 'Da Bush'!"
"Watch out; you'll put yourself in a trick bag."
"Be careful; they'll put in a trick bag."
Da Bush sees some people in office building a street away.
"I've been sitting inside this cubicle all day
with five minutes left on the week I get paid!" said the analyst.
A sound from the next cubicle said, "Bullshit"!
The analyst retorted back; "No bullshit allowed!"
"Bullshit!" said the voice in the next cubicle.
"Fuck ," the analyst got up.
I began walking up to the clerk with an ear piece, asking. "What constitutes as bullshit?"
The clerk, not knowing the escaped Bush is hiding in plain sight answers, "What?"
The analyst responded back, "Bullshit."
"Yea, I get it; but what constitutes bullshit?" the clerk as, while looking at the analyst with concern and confusion; thinking it's possibly better to call security.

The sound, “Bullshit!”
resonated loud enough for the analyst and the clerk to hear. “Bullshit!”
Both the analyst and the clerk move toward the sound saying,
"We calling bullshit!"
As soon as they get to the cubicle, they heard the sound the clerk responds;
"It’s an empty desk with no computer or phone; just a plant?”
The analyst responds, “What is going on here?!” looking at the clerk. The clerk said, "Do look at me…"
"Bullshit!" rings out ; interrupting the rant.
Again, both yell at the same time, “We calling bullshit!”
just as the district manger walked in with clients and asked,
“What kind of peanut gallery is calling bullshit at 10 am?”

Philosophical

Walking one the block one day, just a saying to myself,
'Ooooo!'
"Hey, there!" She turned and looked at me. I said,
'My baby philosophical,
he gone tell you.'
"What?"
'My baby is so philosophical,
he will tell you.'
"What!?"
'My baby is so philosophical,
he gonna tell you the truth.'
"Really?!"
'Yeap!
Even if it hurts, oooooo!'
'And, it it bad of me; that I agreeeee!'
She frowned and said, "Naw.."
I said, 'Is it better from him, or is it better from me?'
'Ooooo!'

Besties II "When Rita made it to work."

"My apologies for being late.
The weather is a mess."
This traffic is a mess; my friends are a mess, yet
I look good as hell. She is looking at herself using her phone.
Responding back an operating room surgeon asks,
"What happened? You were supposed to meet me before your shift."
"I got caught up with one of my closest friends," Rita mentions.
"Is everything alright?"
"Yeah! She's at my place recovering; if anything she should be resting. She was shot at by some guys wife."
"Damn! What do she be getting into?"
Dick is laughing with a little snort and smiles. He snorts when he laughs.
"I wouldn't worry about that; it's kinda cute."
"You really think so?" asks Rita.
Laughing, she playfully hits him on the arm.
Walking into an unassuming and empty patient room,
they passionately slip each other tongue; caressing in
an embrace that could lead to employment termination if caught.
"Damn, I want you!" "I want you too; but I'm late! For work that is."
"I know shit. I know."
"I tell you what; how about we meet in the cafeteria,
and you can tell me about your weekend."
"Are you sure it? Could be considered shocking."
"Well… shock me."
"I got a better idea, Rita suggests. "There is a grand opening at an adult store." The janitor comes in, a bit shocked looking at them, and he is someone that they recognize.

"Ayeee, what up? What you doing up in here? "
"Nothing," says Dick snorting.
“Oh, yea I see now.” says the janitor.
While walking out leaving Dick with the janitor;
Rita rolls her eyes and says, “What’s good; how are you?”
"Ain’t that cute; y’all hanging out at a sex shop."
"I know y’all old school. The DVD and VHS is in the back,"
the janitor states.
Dick shakes his head laughing and leaving
a fifty dollar bill on the table and says,
"You didn’t see anything. By the way she
asked me before I asked her."
Four hours later, both of them left work driving in
separate cars heading to the adult store.
Entering the store, a store attendant greets them.
"Welcome to our grand opening."
"We got everything you would want; just close your eyes, and wish
for it. Hi. I’m Tiffany, but you can call me Tiff."
"Our movie selections are on the right and left corners, and
the center leads you to the matinee rooms; but you are
forbidden to have flash drives."
Rita looks at her puzzled.
“Flash drives? Ain’t nobody trying to down load nothing.”
In a secret hush tone,“Huh? Why you whispering?” Dick asks.
Tiff smiles, “ You’ll be surprised at what the hell people do.”
"May we have two tickets please? It doesn’t matter what.”
asks Dick.

"Sure thing ,"says Tiffany, as she works the register.
"Oh, mmm y'all trying to catch the matinee?" With a slight giggle, she smiles.
"The main theater's free; but you want that private theater that's $50.With that you get to watch two, two hour movies ; and it has a private bathroom with sodas and snack machines.
Unless y'all don't mind sharing a movie with other people. Y'all might like that there; ain't nothing wrong with it. Don't worry I ain't going say nothing."
"Who am I gonna tell?"
As Dick and Rita walk towards the $50 show, they can hear Tiffany say, "Newbies."

This weekend. Love

This weekend, Love.
Beep beep!
Let's hit the highway.
Yes I'm going your way.
Which other way is loose.
Through all the clothes in the caboose.
We heading out from here Baby.
Just as soon as the the weekend comes.

Let set it off somewhere else.
Let's plan the great escape.
Be on time and don't be late.
Got a a make a quick getaway.
Let's plan the great escape.
Let's get a weekend away.

Exhausted from a long week, just clocked out.
Placed the background noise on mute.
No.
Electronics no nothing.
Leave it all on mute.
Glanced out the window and the weather is fugly.
Now I just wanna stay wrapped up and snuggly.
With a book and food from a good cook.
I guess that's all it took.
Let's stay here.
Let's plan the great stay in escape.
Wear to favorite pajamas.
Don't mind if you're late.
Maybe next time we can plan the great escape.
Let's plan the great stay in escape.
I know you can't wait
for this weekend, Love.

One on One

I'm blushing from cheek to
cheek. Wanna get comfortable
and let your breasts out?
I agree.
I want you to get comfortable
and
let your breast's out.
I second
our
imperfections perfection
as we keep growing
in our relationship.
There is
no doubt
at this moment,
we got this mood,
that atmosphere;
plus us.
Almost forgot these candles;
let's turn the lights out.

On Me

Love for you,.
shouldn't be rare
I like to love and
play dirty, to be fair.
So, place you face
between this pair.

Flirt Drunk

The whiskey's hot; and so are you.
Hello sexy; how are you?
I'm with that smoochy smoo… so
tell me what you wanna do.
Let's make sexy noises like we are
eating sweet and thick pound cake.
May I place my thumb in your pie?
More than a notion; more than a dream.
Absolutely, more than I asked for,
you're everything to me.
I'm a fanatic of your love, kisses and
hugs. I'm on that liquor and I'm feeling a
little silly; but I need to talk to your titties.

Pardon me for my intrusion but
your booty send me an invitation.

I…I said, "Pardon me for my intrusion; but
your booty sent me an invitation."
Smiling, looking you in your eyes, I reply, "I
didn't know if I was actually invited so I was
just sitting back debating; contemplating, but
I'm pretty sure your booty sent me an
invitation."

I wait on your response; patiently, waiting.

Duo

Baby, how you want it?

Baby, how did you did it?

Get it like you want it.

Do you want it.

Where my love?

Let's go there!

I'm all in!

How you want it?

Get it when you get it!

Get it!

Get it, 'cuz it's to feel free!

Luxirous lavish.

Hard, long, smooth,

All up inside me

We can create the perfect sounds

as a dynamic duo.

A Word....

"A read before bedtime?"
'Yes.'
"Well how did it all start?"
'It depends on the perspective.'
'But what is the outcome is more important...'
She was tired of that shit. People always telling her what she did and didn't, ain't and can't do. No one wanted to listen to her at all.
"Hush!" was the last thing she heard.
'Okay,' she said to herself. 'I'm hushing.'
She mentally makes a note of how many times he said that to her.
May not have been those exact words, but when someone
doesn't want to hear it (or, only want to hear themselves)
and do it their way; they
might as well should've said fuck you or shut up and listen in the first place.
She was not having it anymore.
She stood in the doorway of the office suites at the Estates,
her arms folded and eyes closed. Her husband of 32 years
was frantically moving the mouse across the grand oakwood desk.
"I didn't need to hear all that. Just be quiet."
She was too stunned to speak. Her eyes started to get hot.
She told herself to either cry or curse.
"Well..." her voice faded out.
She sat in the high back chair by the door like a customer.
"I don't have time for this or you explaining..."
"I just explained what we've talked about—"
Uh... her love's irritation seemed on ten.
She knew he had a deadline to meet.
"You know what." She gets up and heads to the back patio.
She sits down on the purple chair, and lights the Sage on the matching table.
She was tired.
She was in. The same deadline too. She watches the smoke form from the Sage.
She blows it while saying her affirmation.
The smoke billows out.
She hears him groaning from the office.
She laughs and then sighs.
Maybe I misheard him, or he

misheard me? Reality sunk in and she realized she bends to check on beautiful Husband. But who would check on her?
Guess at the moment she was ready for a bubble bath.
He didn’t have time for no shit. He looked up and she was gone. He had a question to ask her but, didnt know when she had left. By then time he looked up and noticed she was gone, it was two hours later. Damn; she didn’t come back to check on me. Dumbfounded, he could not figure out what happened. He just know she came in from her office and asked if he needed her…or, was it her help? He couldn’t remember; he was too focused on what he was doing. And didn't need to hear anything else.
Husband sat back and scratched his chin. Oh, shit, he thought. Maybe I misheard her? Maybe she misunderstood me? Oh, fuck then. He sighed. Guess he needed to check on his Beautiful Wife.
And make sure he had clean sheets for the guest bed.
His Love, driped in rose scented bubbles from the bubble bath, walked naked to the bedroom. Her Love was already from his shower, his body still slightly wet. On their bed he had clean sheets neatly folded and ready for the guess bed. As much as she hated his attitude, she loved him fiercely. As much as she could get on his nervous, he loved her madly.
Lately, she would’ve had something smart to say, a good comeback or wit remark. But she has been quiet and listening.
Lately, he would’ve had something more to say, but he was quiet and listening.
Sometimes, they would go toe to toe, but rather go 69; some cuddle time then sleep.
'Maybe we need to restart' she thought.
Let’s do it again'. he thought.
But their stubbornness and tiredness took over. "Hey, Baby," he said and looked at her through the mirror. "I don’t even think I asked you how was your day?" He was ready for bed. And the walk down the hallway seemed too long.Thank goodness for that nice steam shower and joint. Guess he was ready for sleep, or the television.
"You didn’t," she thought. But the universe and a nice glass of wine had balanced her. The bubble bath just put her over. Now she was ready for sleep."It went," she replied, and turned her back to him on purpose. No free shimmy for him tonight. No pretty nighty or panties, either.

He saw her pull out the old holey black and green sleeper dress.
He already knew what was up. He understood, because he slept nude but opted for some baggy jogging pants and an old muscle shirt.

Slowly, he sighed.
Gently, she rolled her up hair.
Generally, he loved her hair down. But the messy bun gets him hard, too.
Then, she puts on the infamous jumbo orange sleep cap.
Yet, she is still sexy…

She felt his eyes watching her; but she continued to get ready for bed.
Yes, she knew he loved the scented
body oil she makes; but hey, tonight is not the night.
Besides he was wearing those jogging pants that she pretended to
hate, but loved when he wore them.
Damn, these man! He still on my nerve a
little, but I would fuck the shit out of him now.
Nope.She placed on the bonnet and turned off her night stand lamp.

"Night."
"Night." 'Damn she is going to bed this early?' he thought.
He sighed and got his pillows from the side of their bed.
This was going to be the longest walk to the guest room ever.
Well, at least he could stretch out; but that is nothing compared to the warm of the his wife's body. Her breast like cozy pillows; and he
"loved to put himself on her backside.
He loved to drive his hands and tip around the silk and slick curves.
But not tonight.

"Night."
"Night."
'Damn, no kiss? Guess he really is seeing himself to guest room?'
No cuddle love tonight.
She was spoiled of his love.
Just as much as she loved holding him,
pressing her hard nipples and soft warm tummy agains his backside.
She enjoyed his hands rubbing her nipples.
Tongue on her neck.
The hardness inching down her backside
But not tonight.

Hate going to bed upset with each other.
But what are row stubborn people to do?

What could be done together was done separately and silly…

They tossed.

They turned.
She moaned.
He groaned.
They hated going to bed upset with each other.
All they wanted to do was hold each other.
Quietly, he sat still on the guest
bed, and listened for her footsteps. She went to bedroom
door, and listened for his footsteps

Silence..but the hearts' heard.

She left their bedroom.
He left the guestroom.
Somewhere, they meet in the middle of the hallway.
Instead of talking they, embraced and held each other.
Feeling all the good, bad, and indifferent emotions from earlier.
Conversations that were had until morning.
He picked her up and carried her to their bedroom.
She cuddled her face in his neck.
Slowly, he places her on their bed.
She started to take off her clothes; and he did the same.
"I hate it when we fight," he whispered.
"I hate it when we fight as well," she whispered
back letting her emotions and tears flow.
He wiped away her tears; his eyes got misty.

"So," as the Lady concludes the story time for her Gentleman.
She closes the book, and replaces it on her nightstand.
Slowly, she turns back towards him.
They kiss, and then they start to undress each other.
"Sometimes, too many things get in the way
of your life and the love for each other.
Moral of the story is just listen and conversate.
And, don't assume just get some ass."

Close

Feelings of exhilaration overtakes one's thinking;
and they start to drinking
in the fresh water of words.
You can take a stanza out of a book;
but can you dig it as chorus to a song?
I didn't think wrong to ask, did I?
You seem too hesitate too much;
and laugh at mayhem so more.
Yet, you are exhilarated
as you close this book.

Again

(Again and again)
Again and again.
Again and again.
Again and again.
Again and again.
(Again and again)
I want you to kiss me, again and again.
When you kiss me, again and again
I want you to hold me, again and again
I want you to love on me, again and
again. Until the sunrise.
Again and again.
Then,
again and again
Then, you gonna hold me.
Again and again.
You gonna love on me, again and again.
And, always
Again and again.
Good gracious.
I don't know.
I got the beat.
I got the rhyme
lines running through my mind.
Getting
myself together.
Here I go, again and again

Naughty

My rose petal what do you want me to stimulate
more; your labia or your vulva?
Tell me.
What will supercharge you like a nova?
Tell me.
What do I supposed to say or do to capture
a tingling sensation from you?
Tell me.
Place me in the direction you want me to go.
How dare you withhold this passion from yourself.
Naughty.
Or, am I just tawdry with your emotions?
Like your love; your lust I must kiss.
Naughty.
You still want me to play in between your enticement?
Naughty.
Nine different lips.
Are you for that? But, you like it.

Moonlight Wish

I want everyone in the world to wish upon the moonlight and feel good.
Perhaps a party for a momentary break from stress; grab a vibe ,feel the grooves; hangout with strangers; acquaintances; and friends. Then stroll off with, “Until we meet again”.
Rather not, actually, you're accepted time made things different.
It seems kinda distant; just seeing and doing faded bonds;
reminiscing, "No they didn't?" and, "Yes, they diiiiid!!!"
Not in the now; but what the past had did.
Don’t you just hate it?
I’d rather apologize about why I didn’t make it.
On the inside and outside, we're still good for keeping shining lights.
Comfy, happy, chill’n cool, that can be debated; but not argued.
Can you feel the sun shining so bright?
Wish upon the moonlight kiss; passion whispers sweet nothings of love.
Touch the heart of a world in emotional need.
To ask upon me what it means to answer a need.
I reply we as a world succeed at what we want.
My dear world, did you listen or, missed the moment?
"Yes, we did!" "No, we didn’t! " Truly listen.
Everything you ever wished for,
a wish by the moonlight; I wish I may, I wish I might.
Make a wish by the moonlight.

Epilogue

Love is the greatest pain anybody can ever ask for.

Message to Reader

I’m trying to love you; but you not trying to hear my song.
I said I’m trying to love you babe; but you ain’t trying to hear my song.
Because while I’m trying to tell you, babe; you just told me to get my ass on.
Anyway.
Recline with your woofers; and quench your thirst for literature with refreshing narratives cocktails, 'KDLPC' is serving groove chilled stories with infectious and frothy tempos.

About The Authors

Kalisha D. Lemmitt- Cherry
Born and raised in Saint Louis, MO, she is an author, songwriter; producer, publisher, artist, and co- founder of the musical group; "KDLPC" with Peter Cherry. Kalisha has obtained a Bachelor of Arts in English; Certificate in Creative and Technical Writings (University of Missouri-Saint Louis) and Master of Education in Adult and Higher Education (University of Missouri- Saint Louis).
In 2000, she started freelancing and tutoring in various areas.
In 2008, she co-hosted a web-based music radio show, "Soul Therapy," with Peter Cherry. She is also the Owner and CEO: "Serenity Writing and Editing Services, Inc" (est. 2011); and COO of Angelic Reign Inc. (2016).

Peter Cherry

A Saint Louis, MO native, he is an author, songwriter; producer, publisher, artist, co- founder of the musical group; "KDLPC" with Kalisha D. Lemmitt-Cherry. He established "Angelic Reign, Inc." publishing company in 2004.In 2008, he co-hosted a web-based music radio show, "Soul Therapy," with Kalisha D. Lemmitt-Cherry.

Peter has obtained:

Associates Degree in Communications
(St. Louis Community College at Florissant Valley).

Bachelor of Science in Media Studies
(University of Missouri Saint Louis)

Master of Arts in Counseling
(Lindenwood University)

Auto

-Bonus-

I’m up writing this in my sleep.
You're slow dancing with yourself while watching me.
I drift and dream of clits; sensually imagining tickling those milfs...
Oh, so
sweet; moving that ass; shake and drop; feeling it soul deep.
Exquisitely, exciting hearts racing like our loves on the run.
Quenching your thirst; placing my love on your tongue.

In the vibe

www.ingramcontent.com/pod-product-compliance
Lightning Source LLC
Chambersburg PA
CBHW030418310726
48979CB00007B/1101

* 9 7 9 8 9 9 0 2 5 7 8 6 3 *